Worms

by Ann Ruffell

Enty level

Acknowledgements

Cover design: Oliver Heath, Rafters Design

Illustrations apart from pages 5 and 19 © Paul Gardiner, 2005. The right of Paul Gardiner to be identified as the illustrator of this work has been asserted by him in accordance with the Copyright, Design and Patents Act, 1988.

Brinsford books are a direct result of the findings of a two-year authoring/research project with young offenders at HMYOI Brinsford, near Wolverhampton. Grateful thanks go to all the young people who participated so enthusiastically in the project and to Judy Jackson and Brian Eccleshall of Dudley College of Technology.

First published in Great Britain by Axis Education Ltd

ISBN 1-84618-003-1

Axis Education PO Box 459
Shrewsbury SY4 4WZ

Email: enquiries@axiseducation.co.uk

www.axiseducation.co.uk

"Don't look now, but that is so disgusting."
Kerry was on holiday with her boyfriend, Dean. There was a family with kids at their B&B. Dean called them the Slobbers because of their round, sweaty faces.

The oldest boy grinned at Dean.
"Hi. I'm Greg," he said.
Then he lifted a corner of his meat pie. He pulled out something long and wriggly. Then he put it in his mouth.
"I am going to be sick," said Kerry.
"He is just a boy," said Dean. "Don't look."

Today they were going to bike along the trail. Kerry wanted to go off the trail but there was a sign: KEEP OUT.

"What is that place?" said Kerry.

Dean looked at the sign. "It is a lab. It does not say what for."

On the trail there were a lot of frogs. They were not normal.

"I think they have a virus," said Dean. "They should not do that."

"I don't like it here," said Kerry. "Let us go back."

But there was a slope. Her bike slipped on the hill. It was like riding on ice. She crashed into the bushes. Dean slipped too.
The ground was like grease.

They saw Greg, the boy from the B&B.
"There is that Slobber boy," said Kerry. "I bet it is him."
"Just wait until I catch him," said Dean.

"We must warn people," said Kerry. "They will all fall off their bikes."

Dean found a flat piece of wood on the ground.

On the other side it said KEEP OUT.

"Someone has already tried to warn people," he said.

"There are more frogs," said Kerry. "Look – they are all over the place. Perhaps it is not the boy making the road slimy. I think it is the frogs."

A man came up.

"You should not be here," he said.

"It is not safe."

Kerry gave him the sign that said KEEP OUT.

"We found this on the ground," she said.

"Is it yours?"

The man fixed up the sign again.
He told them where the safe path for bikes was.
Dean shook hands.

After he had gone Dean said, "Look at my hand."
It was slimy. Just like the road. Just like the frogs.
Just like the hand of the man.
"You must wash it off now," said Kerry. "You don't want
to catch that virus."

At teatime they saw the Slobber family again.

Greg had lots of worms and slugs on his plate.

"They must be joke worms," said Dean.

"I don't care," said Kerry. "He is still disgusting."

They went for a walk in the sunset.

It was a good time for a snog.

Dean put his arms round Kerry, but Kerry screamed.

"Are you ill?" she said.

"I am okay," said Dean. "What is wrong?"

His arms were cold and sweaty. His face was running with sweat.

"We have to go away from here," said Kerry. "You are ill."

"What do you mean?" said Dean. "I am all right."

But his face looked just like the Slobber family's faces.

Next morning there was slime in the bathroom.

"You have got the virus," said Kerry. She was scared.

"We must go home and see the doctor."

"Tomorrow," said Dean. "We will go tomorrow."

In the night Kerry got up to go to the toilet.

She looked out of the window.

It was raining. The Slobber family were out there in the dark. They were walking over the grass.

Kerry screamed.

Dean woke up. "What is up?" he said.

Kerry pointed to the window. Her hand was shaking. "Look at them!" she yelled. "They are eating worms!"

"It is okay," said Dean. "They are just having a walk."

"In the rain? In the dark?" said Kerry. "There is something bad happening.

I don't care what you say. Tomorrow we go home."

It did not stop raining.

In the morning the power lines were down. They had no lights. They had no phones. The mobile battery was flat and they could not charge it.

And the car would not start.

"I will walk!" said Kerry. "I am not staying here."

She went back to their room for her case.

She turned to run downstairs, but the youngest Slobber was in the doorway.

"Get away from me!" she yelled. She put out a hand to push him away.

The boy opened his mouth.

He bit off her finger, just as if it was a hot dog.

Kerry yelled for Dean but Dean did not come. She locked their room door. Her hand was bleeding badly.

She had to stop the blood.

She opened the case to find her first aid kit.

She was nearly sick.

Out of the case crawled a long, white flat worm.

She had to get to a doctor quickly.

And she had to find Dean.

She opened the door. There was no one on the stairs. It might be safe now.

Then she saw Greg.

"Look what your brother has done!" screamed Kerry. "I need a doctor!"

"I can get you a doctor," said Greg.

"You think I could trust you? Get out of my way!"

The boy began to say something, but suddenly his parents were there.

They smiled. They had sharp teeth.

"What have you done with Dean?" yelled Kerry.

"I saw him going to the lab," said the boy.

"He would not go there," said Kerry. But she had to believe him.

Maybe Dean had gone to find out what was wrong.

Maybe he had gone to find out about the virus.

The father Slobber grinned. His teeth were green and slimy.

"I am the oldest," he said. "I should have the first bite."

Kerry was terrified.

She had to get away from them. But how? They were all standing in her way.

"Come downstairs," said Greg.

He was talking to his family.

It seemed as if he was helping her.

Kerry slammed the door and turned the key. She took the key out of the lock and put it in her bag. She was safe – for a moment.

The lights went on. Someone had mended the power line.

Kerry plugged in her mobile. She could call for help.

Then she dropped the phone.

She heard a click. And she saw the doorknob turn.

Greg put his round, sweaty face round the door.

"Get away from me!" screamed Kerry.

She grabbed her hair drier. It was still plugged in. She pointed a hot blast of air at his face.

"No!" yelled Greg. "I want to help. I ..."

But Greg's face began to break up. His cheeks split. His mouth opened and his lips cracked.

He pushed his hands out to stop the hot air. But his skin cracked like a biscuit.

Kerry could hear the slap, slap of Slobber feet.

They were coming back up the stairs.

She could not hold them all back with one little hair drier.

She kept the hair drier pointed at Greg.

"Keep out!" she yelled.

But it was Dean. Dean and someone else.

And Dean had the Slobber virus too.

"It is all right," said Dean. "You are safe now."

"Keep away from me!" screamed Kerry.

She pointed the hair drier at Dean.

Then she saw the other man.

He had white clothes on.

He was from the lab.

"He will not harm you," said the man from the lab.

"We have got all the others now."

He told her about the frogs.

They had got out of the lab and had given the virus to people.

People started to be like frogs.

They started to eat worms and slugs.

"But – my finger!" said Kerry.

"They were beginning to get a taste for any live meat," said the man.

"But we have got all the frogs now. The people will get better."

He covered Greg with a blanket. There was an ambulance outside.

They took Kerry to the hospital to stitch up her finger. And the next day Dean and Kerry went home.

"I shall never, never go there again," said Kerry.

Dean was washing the car. He wanted to get rid of all the slime.

He did not see the small frog which slipped out into the garden.